Isla OF ADVENTURE

DEEP IN THE RAIN FOREST

by Dela Costa   illustrated by Ana Sebastián

LITTLE SIMON

New York London Toronto Sydney New Delhi

LITTLE SIMON

An imprint of Simon & Schuster Children's Publishing Division

1230 Avenue of the Americas, New York, New York 10020

First Little Simon hardcover edition May 2023

Copyright © 2023 by Simon & Schuster, Inc.

All rights reserved, including the right of reproduction in whole or in part in any form.

LITTLE SIMON is a registered trademark of Simon & Schuster, Inc., and associated colophon is a trademark of Simon & Schuster, Inc. For information about special discounts for bulk purchases, please contact Simon & Schuster Special Sales at 1-866-506-1949 or business@simonandschuster.com.

The Simon & Schuster Speakers Bureau can bring authors to your live event. For more information or to book an event contact the Simon & Schuster Speakers Bureau at 1-866-248-3049 or visit our website at www.simonspeakers.com.

Series designed by Laura Roode.

Book designed by Laura Roode. The text of this book was set in Congenial.

Manufactured in the United States of America 0323 LAK

10 9 8 7 6 5 4 3 2 1

Cataloging-in-Publication Data is available for this title from the Library of Congress.

ISBN 978-1-6659-3172-4 (hc)

ISBN 978-1-6659-3171-7 (pbk)

ISBN 978-1-6659-3173-1 (ebook)

Contents

ALL ABOUT MIA

◊◊◊◊◊◊◊◊◊◊◊◊◊

Who loved to follow Isla Verde around the island of Sol, was very green, and would simply *not* stop talking?

Mia the iguana!

Isla and Fitz had been sitting on the curb of their neighborhood park when Mia stomped by, grumbling to herself. As soon as she'd spotted Isla, well . . . she'd stayed for a chat.

"The injustice!" Mia cried out. She paced back and forth angrily. "The nerve! The unfairness of it all! Oh, cruel world!"

Isla hid a laugh behind her coconut ice-cream cone. If there were contests to crown the most talkative reptile on the island, Mia would win every single time. But Isla kind of liked that about Mia. You could learn a lot from a reptile.

Fitz groaned on the ground by Isla's leg. Unlike Isla, he did *not* like the eternal chatter.

"It is way too hot outside to be this angry," Fitz said. "What's happening and how does it affect me?"

Isla offered Fitz some of her frozen treat. "Something about another iguana stealing her favorite shady tree spot."

Mia huffed and puffed, her nails click-clacking with each step. "Why, don't you know how sensitive my scales are? It's not like I just wake up looking this beautiful in the morning. I need my shady tree canopy!"

Isla knew a large tree canopy was very important. It kept the ground cool for animals.

"Here's a wild idea," Fitz said. "Just find another tree."

"Fitz is right, Mia," Isla said. "Have you looked to see if a tree near you is up for grabs?"

"On the beach? All taken!" Mia sighed.

That made sense. The beach was a total hot spot.

Suddenly, Fitz straightened up. "Hey, what about the rain forest? My cousin is always moving around in there."

Mia gasped in delight. "Fitz, you are brilliant! Simply brilliant, my dear!"

Fitz winked at Isla. "Oh, I get it from my best friend."

"I could hug you, you adorable gecko!" Mia said.

"Oh, no, no, no." Fitz scurried to Isla
for safety. "I'm not really a hugger."

"It's because my scales aren't glimmering, isn't it? Well, too-dah-loo!" Mia said as she walked away. "I'm off to find the best tree in the entire rain forest! A marvelous canopy! The greenest leaves!"

"Good luck!" Isla called out. "We'd better get going too, Fitz. Mama and the Adventure Shack await."

CHAPTER 2

THE ADVENTURE SHACK

◊◊◊◊◊◊◊◊◊◊◊◊◊

Snuggled on a busy shopping street in town, the Adventure Shack promised the very best Sol had to offer.

The shop was bursting with color and music. Before it was Mama's shop, it had been just an old, boring building without personality. But with a little love, time, and imagination, Mama had created her own magical place.

Now everyone knew to stop by the boat-shaped store for all kinds of fun in the sun.

Isla pushed open the door. A bell chimed as she walked in.

Customers looked through all kinds of brochures, checked out the gift shop, and *ooh*-ed at the large posters on the wall.

Snorkeling lessons! Sightseeing! Dolphin-watching!

Beach balls of all sizes! Swimsuits! Snorkeling gear!

"Whoa, check out all the names they have!" A kid's eyes lit up as he found his name on a key chain. "They have *my* name! Key chains never have my name!"

Isla beamed. "Tell me this isn't the coolest place?"

"I can't say that," Fitz replied. "Because it would be a total lie!"

Mama was at the counter handing change to another happy customer.

"*Hola!*" Isla called out, joining Mama as she finished up. "Flyer passer-outers reporting for duty!"

Fitz saluted Mama with his small hands.

Mama gave Isla a kiss and Fitz a gentle pat. "Great timing, *cielo*! The flyers for our new rain forest tour just arrived. See?"

She lifted a stack of colorful papers that read:

NEW RAIN FOREST ADVENTURES

EXPLORE A GREAT GREEN WORLD OF WONDER AND ENCHANTMENT.

COME LEARN MORE AT **THE ADVENTURE SHACK** WHERE ADVENTURE AWAITS!

"Whoa! These look amazing!" Isla gasped. She was especially proud because it was, after all, her job to draw the illustrations on the flyers.

"Great job, Isla." Fitz dangled from Isla's hair to take a close look. "I think this may be your best work yet."

"You think?" Isla grinned.

"Definitely! But is that me in the corner? Are my eyes *really* that close together?" Fitz turned upside down to get a different view.

"Here's something to protect you from the sun," Mama said. She placed a green Adventure Shack hat on Isla's head. She also gave her a treat bag.

"And for your loyal helper, some frozen bananas."

Fitz hopped on Mama's shoulders and hugged her. "Now we're talking! This place really does have it all!"

TROUBLE IN PARADISE

◆◇◆◇◆◇◆◇◆◇◆◇◆

Isla got started right away with her job.

"Come one, come all!" she shouted, skipping through the busy marketplace. "The Adventure Shack invites you to our brand-new tour deep in the rain forest!"

She handed flyers to shoppers, and shoved a few into open mailboxes and bike baskets.

"Should we use your sticky saliva to stick these on windows?" Isla asked Fitz. "No one will mind, right?"

Fitz inched back. "Uh . . ."

Luckily, a few birds stopped. "Hey Isla! Need help passing around flyers?"

"That would be so helpful!" Isla said, rolling up a few so the birds could grab them with their feet.

As the birds flew off, a lady with a huge sun hat stopped in front of them. "Hello, young lady. What's all this excitement about?"

Isla stood tall. "Step right up to the Adventure Shack, *señora*. We promise you won't regret visiting Earth's oldest ecosystem. Marvel at the butterflies. Discover the secret lives of sloths."

On top of her head, Fitz stretched out his arms to look like wings. "Witness the sneaky little bats."

Isla paused and whispered, "Fitz, you *know* how the bats feel about that. They're so sweet."

Fitz hopped back to her shoulder. "Sorry! I got carried away. I think your mama sprinkled sugar on those bananas."

"Are you talking to that gecko?" the lady asked.

"Oh, yes," Isla said, laughing. "He's my best friend. But never mind that! If you'd like to visit the rain forest, we can help."

"And it's totally safe?" the woman asked nervously, noticing Fitz once again.

Isla gave her a thumbs-up. "There's truly nothing at all to worry about."

"Well, if you say so," the woman

said, eagerly this time. "Why don't you go ahead and sign me up?"

But right when Isla was about to lead her back to the Adventure Shack, a scream stopped everyone cold. "MONSTER! THERE'S A MONSTER IN THE RAIN FOREST!"

"Say what?" Fitz said.

A . . . monster? Had Isla heard right?

The lady in the sun hat chuckled nervously and gave the flyer back. "Oh, you know, I think I can wait a little longer to have fun. Maybe next time."

Isla watched her walk away with quick long strides.

Fitz frowned. "I'm definitely going

through a sugar rush because that kid just said there's a monster."

"MONSTER!" Another girl joined in. "HELP!"

Three kids ran past them screaming.

They found a corner to huddle and catch their breath. Isla watched as a group of people nervously tossed away her amazing flyer.

She gulped. "Oh no, Fitz! This isn't good."

Fitz tried to be helpful. "Maybe it's just the way my eyes are drawn."

But Isla knew this was bad news for the Adventure Shack. Now what if nobody wanted to go? What if everyone stopped going to the Adventure Shack all together?

Whatever was going on, Isla had to find out fast.

ROAR! HISS! SNAP!

◆◆◆◆◆◆◆◆◆◆◆◆◆◆

Notebook . . . pen . . . witnesses. Isla had just what she needed to figure out this mystery.

"Hi, there," she said, approaching the spooked kids. "I couldn't help but overhear something about . . . a monster."

"Y-yes!" a boy with checkered pants shrieked. "We were in the rain forest looking for frogs when *ROAR! HISS! SNAP!* A monster appeared!"

"Uh-huh . . . ," Isla said, scribbling down notes. "And about how long were these roars, hisses, and snaps? Seconds? Minutes? Were they high-pitched, or more like a lost critter looking for its parents?"

The kids looked at one another, confused.

"You gotta speak their language," Fitz whispered. "You know, like a regular kid?"

Isla flipped her page to start over. "Sorry, I meant what did this monster look like? Any details, no matter how big or small, could crack this case open."

A girl with pigtails stepped in. "It was a giant land octopus. It had long arms that wiggled around. Ick!"

"No way! Land octopuses aren't real," said a kid with big round glasses. "It was an alien. I always knew they'd come to Sol first; our stars are too shiny to be *real* stars."

"Whatever it was, it was huge. Like a hundred feet tall," the first boy argued. "It was THAT big."

The kids tripped over one another's words as they tried to add more details. By the end, Isla's notebook and mind were both full.

"Thanks, guys," Isla said, tucking her notebook and pencil back into her pocket. "I'll get to the bottom of this."

◊◊◊◊◊◊◊◊◊◊◊◊◊

Back outside the Adventure Shack, Isla flipped through her notes.

Aliens? A hundred-foot tall creature? An icky land octopus with squiggly tentacles?

Isla sighed. "I can't piece any of this together."

Fitz flopped on his back, already tired. "I just know we'll have to go to the rain forest to find out. But what if it really is something scary?"

Scary meant something different for everyone. Maybe the kids had just been surprised by something they had never seen before. That didn't really mean it was scary.

Isla stood up, dusted off her shorts, and said, "Well, whatever it is, I'm sure a talk will calm it down. Or a few roars, hisses, and snaps."

Fitz sighed. "I'm not getting out of this, am I? Beware, rain forest monster. Determined Isla is on her way."

THE ADVENTURE SHACK

CHAPTER 5

SO MUCH FOR PEACE!

◇◇◇◇◇◇◇◇◇◇◇◇◇◇

Isla didn't waste a single minute before starting her new adventure.

With Fitz on her shoulder, she walked through town and watched as the world changed. The sidewalk gave way to dirt, buildings became overflowing nature, and green was everywhere. The trees were different here too. These trees had thicker trunks and darker leaves.

"There." Fitz pointed to a wooden sign that read SOL RAIN FOREST.

"All right, so here's the plan," Isla said, hands on her hips. "We go in, ask a few questions, and find this so-called monster."

Fitz gulped loudly. "Well, if you say so . . . here we go!"

SOL
RAIN
FOREST

The rain forest was enchanting. Isla
could clearly hear the distant sound of
waterfalls. She felt the gentle hugs of
the wind. Crawling insects stopped to
whisper in their quiet voices.

"I wish I could live here, Fitz," Isla said, taking it all in. "Maybe one day we could have a secret hideout by the waterfalls."

"It *is* pretty peaceful," Fitz agreed. "Everything seems so happy and—"

"Oh, the injustice! The scandal! The unfairness of it all!" a familiar voice cried out.

It was Mia the iguana. Isla had forgotten their reptilian friend was searching for a new home. They found her just ahead, stomping back and forth underneath a tree. And right above her, flying around the canopy was . . .

SQUAWK!

"Well, well," Fabio said as he landed on the marshy ground. "Why am I not surprised to see Isla and Franken-gecko in the middle of this monster madness?"

Fitz slapped a hand over his face. "So much for peace!"

Isla had to admit she was a bit surprised to find Fabio away from his beach. She knew how important his muddy tree home was to him, especially with all his little stolen trinkets.

"What are you doing here, so far away from your treasures?" Isla asked.

Fabio touched a feather to his chest. "Haven't you heard? I am being *silenced*."

Isla frowned. "Huh . . . ?"

Mia huffed angrily. "Oh, Isla, you won't believe it. It's simply terrible. You won't even be able to guess what is happening—"

"If you're upset that Fabio's here, I'm sure I can scare him away," Fitz said.

Mia shook her head. "You see, dear, everyone has rejected the invitation to celebrate my new tree. They're too scared of this so-called rain forest monster."

"And if they're too afraid to show up," Fabio continued, "then who will come to hear me sing?"

Fitz and Isla shared a look of understanding. It made total sense that the two most dramatic animals in Sol would be upset at the idea of zero party guests.

Isla cleared her throat. "Well, we're actually on our way to try and find this monster. Would you both like to join—?"

Mia didn't even let Isla finish. She immediately started to march away. "I absolutely must go! No question about it! I must put a stop to this nonsense!"

Fabio let out a battle caw and followed the reptile.

"I hope the monster has earplugs," Fitz said to Isla. "He'll need double-duty protection from Mia *and* Fabio's nonstop talking."

CHAPTER 6

A FLYING MONSTER?

◇◇◇◇◇◇◇◇◇◇◇◇◇◇◇

Mia and Fabio were speaking so fast with each other, it was hard to keep up.

The iguana looked up at the trees. "See how everything is so empty? Surely, the monster is this way."

Fabio nodded. "I don't hear any twittering birds. Odd, considering a celebrity is here."

Mia stopped. "A celebrity? Where?"

"Me, of course!" Fabio looked a bit offended.

"Oh, of course, of course," Mia replied awkwardly, then quickly resumed walking.

"I can't believe I'm saying this," Isla whispered to Fitz. "But I think these two might be our best bet to solve this case. They work *so* well together."

"I think you're right," Fitz whispered back. "Who would've thought?"

"Now, pay attention," Mia said. "We don't have much time before my party is supposed to start, and a party we must have. It will be the talk of the town if no one shows up. What do we know so far?"

Isla took out her notebook and flipped through. "According to several kids, it's very tall, loud, and . . . scary."

Fabio huffed. "Well, that's not very helpful!"

Fitz ignored him. Instead, he looked around their surroundings.

"Are you guys sure you know where we're going? Because we just went in a circle."

Isla realized Fitz was right. They'd already passed by the same river . . . twice. Could it be they were lost? Then they might really be in trouble.

"I always know where I'm going, sweetkins," Mia said. "I've been to many tree parties around here. Everyone is always begging me to go."

Fabio quickly added his two cents. "Everyone asks *me*, too. They're like, 'Oh, Fabio, you *have* to come sing. It won't be a party without you.'"

The four continued to walk until they finally reached a dead end. Thick hanging vines blocked the way.

"What now?" Fitz asked. "Left? Right? Back home for a nap?"

Mia whipped around. Finally, she confessed, "Darlings, I've always said I'd admit it when I've made a mistake, and I'll admit it now. I absolutely lost track of where we were going while I was talking."

Suddenly, something flew by and they all jumped in surprise.

"AH!" Fitz shouted, nearly falling off Isla's shoulder. "MONSTER! NO ONE SAID IT WAS A FLYING MONSTER!"

CHAPTER 7

IT GREW AND GREW AND GREW

◇◇◇◇◇◇◇◇◇◇◇◇◇◇

Thankfully, the flying creature was not even close to being a monster.

It was a hummingbird. The poor little guy moved in bursts of panic.

His blue-green feathers sparked a memory for Isla. "Hey . . . don't I know you from somewhere? Perry, right? You helped Abuela, Abuelo, and me find fresh honey for baking."

The hummingbird flew up and chirped in surprise. "Isla Verde! I would usually say I'm glad to see you, but heed my warning. Go . . . no . . . further. Something monstrous this way comes."

"That's all the warning I need," Fitz said, sweating nervously. "Let's get out of here!"

Isla clapped her hands together. "That's the best news I've heard all day!"

Fabio flew up to meet Perry in the air. "Tell us, tiny bird, what does this beast look like?"

Suddenly, a deep and low roar echoed throughout the forest. Isla heard the rustling of leaves and something slithering on the ground.

"Eek!" Perry squeaked. "I think that speaks for itself."

Something was definitely, totally, and quickly coming.

"What . . . was . . . that?" Mia whispered.

Perry flew in fast circles. "Is no one else freaking out about this?"

Fitz raised both his hands and his tail.

"Let's hide over here," Isla suggested. She was trying to keep her cool, especially with how nervous her friends were becoming.

The group quickly hid behind a large tree trunk.

The roar came again and was followed by a long hiss.

The friends poked their heads out from the sides of the trunk.

Fabio snorted. "Is this a bad time for me to say that the monster's roar is off-pitch? Can someone say *embarrassing*."

"No one is worried about that right now," Fitz whispered, shushing the laughing seagull.

Fabio stopped laughing when the spooky sounds echoed once more.

"Oh, sweet nectar." Perry shook his head. "I think that's all I can handle. Gotta fly! Good luck, Isla." Perry gave her a quick nod and disappeared in a heartbeat.

It's nothing, it's nothing, Isla repeated to herself. Except . . . it very clearly was something.

They'd heard the roar. They'd heard the hiss.

And now . . . *snap!*

"L-look. Quick. On the vines!" Mia exclaimed.

At first, Isla didn't see anything except the hanging vines and leaves. She squinted her eyes, leaned forward . . . and there.

A shadow, growing from the corner.

It was small at first. Eyes wide and hearts beating fast, the friends watched as it grew, and grew, and grew.

"It's—it's—" Mia stuttered.

Fitz finished, "THE MONSTER!"

The shadow's arms spread out as it hissed angrily. Fitz, Fabio, and Mia screamed.

PULL IT TOGETHER!

◇◇◇◇◇◇◇◇◇◇◇◇◇

Isla pulled Fabio, Fitz, and Mia back behind the tree.

"Shh . . . we've got to stay quiet," she whispered. "Let's watch what it does."

If she could pay attention to how it moved, maybe she'd figure out what kind of animal was scaring everyone. If there was anything Isla had learned in all her years of speaking with animals, it was that misunderstood creatures could *seem* scary. That didn't mean they were.

But her friends weren't really following her train of thought.

Fabio, especially, was frantic. He dropped to his knees and spread his wings dramatically. "Oh, this monster will ruin all of my grand plans! Now no one will come see me perform at the Sol theater. If no one sees my talent, who will name a street after me? Worst of all, I'll never hear my thousands of adoring fans again. Oh, Isla, I never told you this, but . . . I love it when you chase me around. It's our thing. Our shtick. No one does it like us."

Fitz smacked Fabio with his tail. "Fabio, no one ever chases you."

Fabio pulled Fitz into a tight hug. "Come here, you. Oh, Fitzgerald, you're my very best friend. Now . . . we shall face this beast together as one. A mighty team. Bird and reptile. Your little sticky feet and my fabulous wings."

"H-help," Fitz wheezed, unable to breathe.

Oh, how Isla wished she had a camera!

"Boys, please," Mia said. "Will you pull it together?"

HISSSSSSSSSSSSS! SNAP!

"There's that hiss and snap sound again," Isla said, trying to see just where it was coming from. "The monster sounds pretty close . . . but I can't see anything besides its shadow. Do you guys see anything?"

Mia stretched her
neck. In a quiet
voice she replied,
"Darling, I see
nothing. But I am
very close to the
ground, I'm afraid to
say. Can't see much."

Isla quickly thought about all the
things people claimed the monster was.
She knew it couldn't be a hundred-foot
tall monster. Surely
they would have
seen it by now.

It couldn't be a land octopus because there would be tentacle prints in the dirt.

Plus, she'd never met a hissing rain forest octopus. That just wasn't a thing.

And aliens? Well, Isla hadn't read enough about that subject to know much.

CROAK! CROAK! CROAK!

Wait a minute, she thought. *Is that a croak?*

"It's getting closer," Fitz said, shaking. "Isla, is this the part where we run screaming like those kids?"

The shadow grew taller and taller,
arms long and wiggling.

"LAAAAA!" Fabio sang loudly. "THE MONSTER IS UPON US!"

"Isla, dear," Mia said nervously. "Maybe the boys are right. . . ."

Just as Isla was about to grab her animal friends and make a run for it, she heard yet another unexpected sound.

"Y-y-yikes," a trembling voice said. "Did you hear that, Barry? The monsssster is here."

Another voice added, "Well, geesh, Doug. Don't get its attention."

"O-oh," Doug replied. "You're right. *Hissssss*."

"Guys," Isla said to her friends, "I think there's something else here with us. And they sure are doing a whole lot of hissing."

CHAPTER 9

DOUG AND BARRY

◇◇◇◇◇◇◇◇◇◇◇◇◇

Mia gasped and pointed with a long nail. "There! Look at the bushes near the vines."

Isla followed Mia's nail to a pair of large, leafy bushes. The first thing she noticed was how one of them was trembling so much that leaves fell out in bunches. Next, she saw a tiny head with big black eyes pop out.

It was a frog.

The tiny critter looked left and right. "I don't see anything yet, Doug. We might be able to sneak out of here."

From the trembling leafy bush, another head popped out. It belonged to a beautiful blue snake. "A-are you sure, Barry?"

"Oh yeah, buddy," Barry replied. "Trust my froggy instincts."

Isla looked from the scary shadow . . . to Barry and Doug's movements . . . back to the shadow. . . . The long, thin shape was shaking just as hard as Doug's lean snake body. And when Barry stretched his little arms, so did the shadow.

Isla moved away from the tree and toward them. "Hello."

As soon as Doug spotted her, the snake ducked back into the bushes. "MONSSSSTER!"

"Monster? Who are you calling a monster? The guts on you," Mia said, joining Isla. "Just because she doesn't have scales and has hair coming out of her head doesn't make her a monster."

Barry watched the friends curiously. "It's just a *girl*. And a bird . . . a gecko . . . and an iguana. Hm. What a weird group. Definitely weird, but not at all scary."

Fabio pushed Fitz away and sputtered.

"Bird? Who are you calling a bird? I'm a *seagull*," Fabio clarified.

"You're loud, is what you are," Barry said. "Don't you know we're hiding from a monster? *CROAK!*"

Barry's croak echoed louder than Isla would've thought possible. A smile spread across her face as the pieces started to come together.

At the same time, a look of understanding crossed Fitz's eyes. "Wait a minute . . . that croak . . . are YOU two what everyone's been so scared of?"

Fabio flew to the shadow, inspecting its shaking. "Without question. These two nearly kept the world from hearing my voice."

Doug popped back out. "H-huh?"

"Now that's just froggy talk," Barry

said. "See, Doug and I were minding our own business slithering around, looking for lunch or whatnot. When suddenly, a bunch of kids started screaming that they saw a monster. We've been hiding in these bushes ever since."

103

Isla kneeled to get closer. "I think you might've accidentally scared those kids. See how your joined shadows move? It looks kind of . . . creepy. No offense."

Doug and Barry looked at their shadows, then jumped in surprise.

"Yikes!" Barry said. "That shadow's worse than my croak."

"Oh no. We didn't mean to scare anyone," Doug said. "Sssnake's honor, we swear we didn't."

Isla smiled. "If anything, you've added a little mystery and adventure to Sol's rain forest."

Barry's stomach growled. "We haven't eaten all day because of this monstrous misunderstanding."

Mia came to the rescue. "Oh, darlings, this must be your lucky day. I'm officially inviting you to my party as my guests of honor! Just think of it . . . the rain forest monsters at *my* party."

"All right." Barry did a high-five with Doug's tail.

"Will there be lots of food?" Fitz asked.

"Only the absolute best," Mia said. "But remember—BYOL."

Isla frowned. "I'm not sure what that means."

"Bring your own lettuce," Fabio said. "Duh."

CANOPY PARTY

◊◊◊◊◊◊◊◊◊◊◊◊◊◊

Mia's party was a total success. It was the first rain forest party Isla had ever been invited to, and she hoped it wouldn't be the last. Iguanas from all over the island showed up. And yes, they brought their own lettuce.

Isla brought a blanket from home and a tub filled with fresh lettuce and fruit. Fitz was already on his second mango.

A toucan perched high on a tree and was telling jokes. Butterflies floated above like confetti. Even the Tree Frog Choir stopped by.

Fabio wasn't thrilled to be sharing a stage, but they made it work.

"This is quite the party," Mia said, joining Isla on her blanket. "Thank you, darling, for all your help."

"Of course. How's the lettuce?" Isla asked. She'd picked the best lettuce leaves from Mama's backyard garden.

"Crunchy," Mia said, taking a bite of a leaf. "I must say, I'm glad to be away from the toucan. Have you ever heard such a chatty animal?"

"Oh no," Fitz joked. "Not at all."

"Got room for us?" Doug and Barry appeared from behind bushes. But this time, no one ran away screaming.

Instead, Mia cleared her throat to gather her other guests closer. "Here they are. May I introduce the monsters of the rain forest, Doug and Barry."

"Oh my!" a group of iguanas chattered, gossiping away. "You two sure gave everyone a fright. Is it true you can become a hundred feet tall?"

Doug showed off his small frog muscles. "My mother always told me that if I stretched enough every day, I could become as tall as Doug here."

"And has it worked?" Fitz asked, frowning.

"Are you kidding?" Barry exclaimed. "Look at how much taller we both are when I stretch."

The iguanas laughed and Mia winked.
"I'm glad you two finally showed up.
I have a surprise." Isla pulled out a folded
piece of paper from her pocket. "Check
out the newly designed Adventure Shack
rain forest flyer."

Barry and Doug's eyes widened. She had drawn them next to Fitz.

Doug hissed happily. "We're famousss, Barry."

"And my eyes finally look right!" Fitz cheered.

Isla and her animal friends spent the rest of the time chatting, coming up with goofy monster names, and sharing lettuce. If that wasn't what living in Sol was about, Isla didn't know what was.

DON'T MISS ISLA'S NEXT ADVENTURE!

HERE'S A SNEAK PEEK!

◆◆◆◆◆◆◆◆◆◆◆◆◆◆

"Isla, you've got snail mail!"

Isla Verde looked up from her desk. She was in the middle of reading about different leaves on the island of Sol. Sol, her beautiful island home, was filled with many, many types of plants. It was as if the land shifted and made room for more to grow.

Putting the book down, Isla swirled around in her desk chair.

"You're always a welcome break,

Mama," Isla said. "I wonder if it's my new magnifying glass."

"I don't think it would fit in this." Mama placed two envelopes on Isla's desk. "One for you and one for Fitz. Take a look while I finish making lunch."

As Mama left, Isla's best gecko friend leaped up from his nap. "Mail from snails is the worst! Remember that one time we brought them apples and they sent us back an envelope full of leftovers?"

Isla shivered. How could she forget the soggy envelope? "Those leftover apples had seen better days. But I don't think Mama meant *that* kind of snail mail. These letters were delivered by someone on foot."

Fitz sniffed the air. "These don't *smell* like old apples. . . ."

They studied the envelopes. One was bright pink and had Isla's name written on it in big, glittery letters. The other one was much smaller and had Fitz's name spelled out with stickers.

"Who would send us such bright, glittery envelopes?" Isla asked, winking at Fitz.

"I'm no detective," Fitz replied. "But I think I know who this is from. . . ."

At the same time, they exclaimed, "Tora!"

"Let's open them!" Fitz said.

Isla opened his first and then hers. Even more glitter spilled out from inside the envelopes as they took out invitations. They read:

**YOU ARE INVITED TO
THE ULTIMATE SLEEPOVER
EXTRAVAGANZA
WHERE: THE ROSA HOUSE (NEXT DOOR)
WHEN: TONIGHT! EEEEEP!
BRING: FUN PJS AND YOURSELF, PLEASE!**

Fitz whistled, shaking some glitter off his feet. "She sure knows how to sell a party. Even though I don't know what an *eggs*-tra-va-gan-za is . . . do you?"

Isla spelled it out for him on a piece of paper. "It's *ex*-tra-va-gan-za. It means a huge party!"